The Boy with the Sweet-Treat Touch

By Laura North
Illustrated by Neil Chapman

Crabtree Publishing Company
www.crabtreebooks.com

Crabtree Publishing Company
www.crabtreebooks.com
1-800-387-7650

616 Welland Ave.
St. Catharines, ON
L2M 5V6

PMB 59051, 350 Fifth Ave.
59th Floor,
New York, NY 10118

Published by Crabtree Publishing Company in 2015

First published in 2013 by Franklin Watts
(A division of Hachette Children's Books)

Text © Laura North 2013
Illustration © Neil Chapman 2013

Series editor: Melanie Palmer
Series advisor: Catherine Glavina
Series designer: Peter Scoulding
Editors: Jackie Hamley, Kathy Middleton
**Proofreader and
   notes to adults:** Shannon Welbourn
**Production coordinator and
   Prepress technician:** Margaret Amy Salter
Print coordinator: Katherine Berti

Printed in Hong Kong/082014/BK20140613

To Tehya - LN

**Library and Archives Canada
Cataloguing in Publication**

North, Laura, author
     The boy with the sweet-treat touch / by Laura
North ; illustrated by Neil Chapman.

(Race ahead with reading)
Issued in print and electronic formats.
ISBN 978-0-7787-1461-3 (bound).--
ISBN 978-0-7787-1364-7 (pbk.).--
ISBN 978-1-4271-7782-7 (pdf).--
ISBN 978-1-4271-7770-4 (html)

     I. Chapman, Neil, illustrator II. Title.

PZ7.N815Bo 2014   j823'.92   C2014-903701-5
                                   C2014-903702-3

**Library of Congress
Cataloging-in-Publication Data**

North, Laura.
  The boy with the sweet-treat touch / by Laura
North ; illustrated by Neil Chapman.
       pages cm. -- (Race ahead with reading)
  "First published in 2013 by Franklin Watts"--
Copyright page.
   ISBN 978-0-7787-1461-3 (reinforced library
binding) -- ISBN 978-0-7787-1364-7 (pbk.) --
ISBN 978-1-4271-7782-7 (electronic pdf) --
ISBN 978-1-4271-7770-4 (electronic html)
  [1. Birthdays--Fiction. 2. Wishes--Fiction. 3. Magic-
-Fiction. 4. Desserts--Fiction. 5. Greed--Fiction.] I.
Chapman, Neil, illustrator. II. Title.

 PZ7.N8144Bo 2014
 [E]--dc23
                                   2014020700

Chapter One

It was the day before Jack's birthday. He was going to be nine years old. His dad had made him a special cake with nine candles.

"Can I have a piece now?" said Jack, looking at the big cake hungrily.

"No, Jack," said Dad. "You'll have to wait until tomorrow!"

Jack was annoyed. The cake looked so delicious, and he was very greedy. When his dad wasn't looking, he grabbed a huge slice of cake and stuffed it in his mouth.

"Get upstairs to bed, Jack!" shouted his dad. "You're too greedy."

Jack ran up the stairs. He went into his bedroom. Under the bed there was a silver box, glinting in the light.

"I wonder if that's a birthday present for me?" he thought.

He ripped open the silver paper, even though it wasn't his birthday yet. Inside the box was a sparkling gold coin.

There were some words on it: "Touch me and your next wish will come true."

"Yeah, right!" said Jack. "I bet nothing happens at all." He held the coin in his hands, then put it in his pocket and forgot about it. How could a stupid coin make his wishes come true?

Chapter Two

Jack sat down for dinner with his mom and dad. All he could see on his plate was a sea of vegetables. "I hate broccoli," said Jack. "And peas and carrots."

But in the middle of the table was a big chocolate mousse, which was for dessert. "Can I have some dessert now, please?" begged Jack.

"No," said his mom. "You have to finish your broccoli first."

"I hate broccoli!" shouted Jack.

"I wish that I only had to eat treats. I wish that everything I touched could turn into a treat!" Jack grabbed his broccoli and threw it onto the table in a tantrum.

Before his parents could lecture him about being so greedy and badly behaved, something magical happened. **ZAP!** Suddenly his broccoli disappeared.

In its place was a huge cream cake. It was covered in pink icing and raspberries. He quickly stuffed the creamy wonder into his mouth until it was all gone.

"My wish came true!" cried Jack, through mouthfuls of cake. He took the coin out of his pocket. It was glowing brightly.

"I can't wait for my birthday now. My life is going to be amazing—all treats and nothing else!" said Jack.

Chapter Three

The next day, Jack woke up bright and early. "I'm nine years old today, and I have a super power!" he said.

He realized that he had a pile of homework to do. "I haven't even started my math homework," he groaned.

He picked up his textbook.
ZAP! The homework full of
numbers and graphs became
a sundae, with layers of
ice cream, fruit, and chocolate.

"I can tell my teacher I ate my homework!" he said as he stuffed the sundae into his mouth, ice cream dripping down his face. "This has to be the best birthday present ever!" he shouted.

There was a knock at the front door.

"Jack!" shouted Mom. "It's Robert.

He's coming up to play a video game."

The boys sat down in front of the TV

to play a game.

But as soon as Jack touched his controller
it turned into a chocolate eclair.

"Oh well," he said licking his fingers.

"What happened?" said Robert, looking
confused.

"The best thing ever," said Jack.

"Everything I touch turns into a treat."

"Yeah, right," said Robert.

Jack grabbed Robert's controller.

It turned into another chocolate eclair.

Jack ate that one, too.

"I have to go now," said Robert alarmed.

"OK, bye!" called Jack, as Robert hurried

out of his bedroom.

Jack had a weird feeling. He was feeling a bit sick after eating so many treats, and he wished he could have played the game with his friend.

"Oh well," he said. "I've got my party to look forward to now."

Chapter Four

Jack's mom and dad spent hours getting his

party ready. All of his friends came over.

There were balloons, party games, and lots

of brightly wrapped birthday presents all

sitting on the table.

"Here," said his best friend Sarah. "I think you'll love this. I took me forever to find it." Jack grabbed it. But as soon as he started to rip the wrapping paper off...

ZAP! It turned into a big ice cream cone covered with chocolate and marshmallows.

Sarah watched in horror. Jack picked up the presents one by one, and each one turned into a different cake or dessert.

"All of my presents are gone," he said.

The whole room was stuffed full of desserts,

all different sizes and colors.

Sarah looked upset, so Jack went to hug her.

But as soon as he touched her, she turned into a green-and-orange tower of jello with sugar diamonds on top. His wish had turned the best day of his life into a nightmare.

Chapter Five

"I turned my best friend into a dessert,"

Jack cried. "I wish I hadn't been so greedy.

I just want her back."

He put the jello Sarah in the fridge to

make sure no one ate her.

Jack put his hand in his pocket and pulled out the glittering gold coin. "I wish that things would just go back to the way they were!" he cried.

"I promise I will not be greedy or misbehave anymore. Just please turn my friend back." The coin glowed in his hand.

Jack crossed his fingers and ran back down the stairs. All his presents were back on the table, although his new race car had some bite marks in it.

He took a deep breath and went to the
kitchen. He opened the fridge door slowly.
"What am I doing in the fridge?"
said Sarah. She climbed out, shivering.

From that day on, Jack wasn't so keen on treats. And he was very careful about what he wished for.

Make sure the next wish you make is one you won't regret, just in case it comes true...

These entertaining, first chapter books help children build up their reading skills so they can move on to longer books. Fun illustrations and bite-sized chapters encourage young readers to take the driver's seat and *Race Ahead with Reading.*

THE FOLLOWING BEFORE, DURING, AND AFTER READING ACTIVITY SUGGESTIONS SUPPORT LITERACY SKILL DEVELOPMENT AND CAN ENRICH SHARED READING EXPERIENCES:

BEFORE

1. Make reading fun! Choose a time to read when you and the reader are relaxed and have time to share the story together. Don't forget to give praise! Children learn best in a positive environment.
2. Before reading, ask the reader to look at the title and illustration on the cover of the book **The Boy with the Sweet-Treat Touch.** Invite them to make predictions about what will happen in the story. They may make use of prior knowledge and make connections to other stories they have heard or read about someone with a special power or another similar character.

DURING

3. Encourage readers to determine unfamiliar words themselves by using clues from the text and illustrations.
4. During reading, encourage the child to review his or her understanding and see if they want to revise their predictions midway. Encourage the reader to make text-to-text connections, choosing a part of the story that reminds them of another story they have read; and text-to-self connections, choosing a part of the story that relates to their own personal experiences; and text-to-world connections, choosing a part of the story that reminds them of something that happened in the real world.

AFTER

5. Ask the reader **who** the main characters are in this story. Have the child **retell** the story in their own words. Ask him or her to think about the predictions they made before reading the story. How were they the same or different?

DISCUSSION QUESTIONS FOR KIDS

6. Throughout this story, Jack is greedy and badly behaved. How does he change his behavior to improve the outcome of the story?
7. Choose one of the illustrations from the story. How do the details in the picture help you understand a part of the story better? Or, what do they tell you that is not in the text?
8. What part of the story surprised you? Why was it a surprise?
9. Jack makes a wish on the sparkling gold coin. What would you wish for if you were Jack?
10. What moral, or lesson, can you take from this story?
11. Create your own story or drawing about something you would wish for and how it would change your life.